Lexi's Tale

· *A Park Pals Adventure* ·

Johanna Hurwitz

ILLUSTRATED BY

Patience Brewster

SeaStar Books
NEW YORK

For Andrea Spooner,
who knows how to improve a tale
par excellence
—J. H.

Text © 2001 by Johanna Hurwitz
Illustrations © 2001 by Patience Brewster

SEASTAR BOOKS
A division of NORTH-SOUTH BOOKS INC.

First published in the United States by SeaStar Books, a division of North-South Books Inc., New York. Published simultaneously in Canada, Australia, and New Zealand by North-South Books, an imprint of Nord-Süd Verlag AG, Gossau Zürich, Switzerland.

Library of Congress Cataloging-in-Publication Data is available.
The artwork for this book was prepared by using pencil.
The text for this book was set in 16-point Centaur MT.

ISBN 1-58717-091-4 (reinforced trade binding)
1   3   5   7   9   RT   10   8   6   4   2

Printed in U.S.A.

For more information about our books, and the authors and artists who create them,
visit our web site: www.northsouth.com

CONTENTS

CHAPTER ONE
Breakfast in the Park

What's better than being a squirrel: running, leaping, soaring, and flying through the air? Being a squirrel means eating delicious seeds and nuts, fruits and flowers, mushrooms and plant buds, and all sorts of leftovers from humans. Being a squirrel means wearing a warm and handsome coat of fur and waving a magnificent tail. What's better than being a squirrel? Nothing!

My name is Lexington, but those who know me best save time by calling me Lexi. Lexington is also the name of a big street in New York City where I live. Most of my squirrel relatives are named after streets too. Perhaps that's why I and all my family are so street-smart. There's my brother Madison and my cousins Amsterdam and Columbus, for example. But just as most city streets are named by numbers, so most of my relatives are called by those numbers too. I have sisters named Sixty-one, Sixty-two, and Sixty-three, to mention just a few.

From my home, in a hole high in a maple tree in Central Park, I can see just about everything. I watch the birds flying about and I check out the morning as the park begins to fill with human visitors. At dawn today, I looked out and saw a lone man with a dark beard walking back and forth, back and forth, on a nearby path. He wasn't wearing running clothes or running shoes, like most early-morning visitors to the park. He had a cap on his head, but it wasn't a baseball cap. On his feet, instead of sneakers, he wore a pair of leather sandals with socks. I've noticed that when people wear sandals, they generally let their bare toes stick out. And, the man seemed to be talking to himself. Silly, I thought.

"Lexi," a voice called to me. "How many squirrels are in this park?"

I looked down from my perch. Below me stood

a fat, tailless creature. It was PeeWee, my guinea pig friend. Many weeks ago, at the time of the full flower moon, he was abandoned in the park by his former owner.

"Who can count? And who cares?" I raced down the tree and landed on the ground next to PeeWee.

"Everywhere I look, I see squirrels," PeeWee said. "There must be hundreds of squirrels around here."

"I know that years ago a scientist, with nothing better to do with his time, came and spent many weeks trying to count," I said. "My old uncle Ninety-nine heard the fellow say that there were more than thirteen thousand eight hundred squirrels here in the park. My uncle laughs when he talks about it because he knows there are loads more squirrels than that."

What my guinea pig friend didn't know was that back when he first arrived in the park, Uncle Ninety-nine warned me to keep away from him.

"Squirrels don't need other animals," he had reminded me. "That fat funny fellow won't be any use to you. In fact, he might get you into trouble."

"He's interesting," I had told my uncle. "He may not be able to climb to the top of a tree, but he's seen other parts of the world. He's lived in a pet shop and inside a human home."

"If you don't watch out, you'll find yourself in one of those places too," old Uncle Ninety-nine had warned me as he dug in the ground. Luckily he had found a large nut and become so busy eating it that he had forgotten what he was saying. My uncle is enormous. All squirrels love food and we eat our own body weight each week, but Uncle Ninety-nine seems to eat enough for two squirrels. As a result, he's almost as big as some of the dogs that come walking in our park.

"It must be great fun to have such a huge family," PeeWee said to me, as he has more than once, referring to the large number of squirrels and not the large size of my uncle.

"Squirrels don't care very much about family," I told him. "We don't mate for life like many other animals do. Father squirrels don't stick around to help raise their children. And babies become independent at a very young age. We may play together and chase one another, but a squirrel looks after himself." I gave myself a good scratch as I thought about it some more. "No," I added, "squirrels never go out on a limb for anyone else."

"You don't know how lucky you are," said PeeWee sadly. "I wish there were at least one other guinea pig in the park."

Poor PeeWee. I hadn't given the matter much thought before, but now I realized that it must be lonely to be the only representative of your species in all the 843 acres that make up Central Park. Even the animals over in the zoo are paired together. I tried to distract him.

"Cheer up," I said. "If you were back inside that old cage you used to live in, you wouldn't have another guinea pig or even a squirrel like me to keep you company."

"You're right," PeeWee quickly agreed. "What would I have done without you?"

I didn't answer. The truth is, without me, he

never would have survived in the park from day one. PeeWee would have starved or been caught by a dog or come to some other dreadful fate. He arrived in the park with no survival skills at all. He didn't know how to climb a tree. He'd never dug for food or hidden from danger before. He still can't climb trees, but at least he's learned the other things that he needs to live in the outside world. And PeeWee did come to the park with one very special talent: He knows how to read. That's right, read! He's the only animal I've ever heard of who can do that. And so many times, when other squirrels are sleeping in their nests or chewing on a pawful of seeds, I sit in his little hole and listen to the stories that he reads aloud from the books and papers that have been left in the park by careless humans.

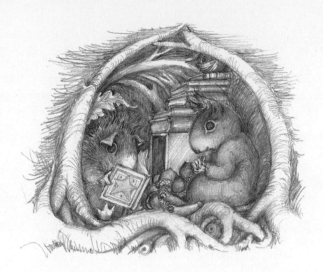

"We're living in paradise," I told PeeWee. "Don't forget it."

"You're right," he agreed with me again. "This park has just about everything, even if it doesn't have other guinea pigs. The food here is a hundred times better than my old cage food. I can't believe that I was once satisfied eating little dry pellets."

"Speaking of food," I said, "I haven't eaten my morning meal yet. Have you?"

"No," PeeWee said.

"Then let's not waste our time talking when we can be chewing," I told him. "Remember what my mother always said: *Early to rise, early to dig, makes a squirrel happy, healthy, and big.*"

"Guinea pigs too," said PeeWee, pulling a perfect apple out of a pile of leaves where some foolish human must have thrown it. There were no apple trees nearby, and besides, it was far too early in the season for the park's apple trees to be growing fruit.

"Come and have a bite or two," PeeWee called to me.

What a friend! PeeWee is always quick to share whatever he's eating. Squirrels never share. All squirrels seem to fear that the nut they're eating is the last they'll ever see. Our only sharing is by chance. We all bury extra nuts and seeds, and when we relocate them, we rarely know if they are actually the ones that we hid or if they were buried by a relative instead. It seems to balance out, however. There's always something good to eat hidden beneath the soil.

I heard the rustle of footsteps on the ground nearby and looked up from the apple PeeWee and I were sharing. Coming toward us was the bearded man I'd noticed earlier. "Hide," I whispered to PeeWee. "There's someone coming. You mustn't be seen."

At once PeeWee scooted under a nearby bush. It wouldn't do for a human to see a guinea pig here in the park. But no one seems to notice us squirrels. There is a definite advantage to being part of such a large population. I climbed partway up the maple tree and watched.

The man walked past. He wasn't talking now, but his head was down and he seemed to be looking for something. To my amazement, he reached down and picked up the apple that PeeWee had dropped. He brushed off some dirt and took out a small pocket knife. He trimmed the chewed section of the fruit away and then he took a large bite.

The man walked away munching on my and PeeWee's meal. I shouted angrily at him in my squirrel tongue, but of course he couldn't understand. What did he think he was doing? How awful humans can be, I thought as I began digging for something to take the place of our missing apple. How dare that man steal our breakfast!

CHAPTER TWO

Rehearsal Time

Squirrels may be very independent creatures, keeping to themselves most of the time, but there is one big exception: Once a year we squirrels hold a huge gathering in the park. It's not only my brothers and sisters living nearby who attend; cousins and relatives all journey from the far edges of the park to the affair. They travel from other parks in the city too. On this night we hold our famous Squirrel

Circus so we can all show off our talents at jumping, climbing, balancing, and running. The big event was going to take place just six nights from now.

"How do you know exactly when the circus will be?" PeeWee asked me. He was very curious about it and eager to watch our acrobatics. He reminded me of myself when I was a newborn squirrel, looking forward to my first Squirrel Circus.

"It takes place on the night of the full strawberry moon, even if it rains and the moon can't be seen. We'll gather when the clock strikes ten," I added. I was referring to the hour on the mechanical clock that is a famous park landmark, not my young cousin Ten.

"It's strange to be ruled by human time," PeeWee commented.

He was right about that. Every other day squirrels rise and sleep by the angle of the sun. The weather affects our actions too. But on the day of the Squirrel Circus, we rely on the mechanical clock because its chimes can be heard from a great distance and it will not be silenced by a cloud.

There were two things I had to do before the night of the Squirrel Circus. I had to rehearse my own special act, and equally important, I had to deliver the foods that I was contributing to the feast that would follow the gymnastics.

For the past couple of days more squirrels than usual had been rushing about carrying nuts or seeds in their mouths. The food was being stored up for the banquet in three centrally located tree holes. I wondered how so many squirrels could be in one area of the park without any humans noticing.

Then PeeWee reminded me that I had once told him that all humans looked more or less alike to me. He'd said, "Did you ever think that humans may feel that way about squirrels?" PeeWee was right. The people who were nearby would never know if they'd seen three squirrels or thirty.

Up in my tree hole I had put a half-full box of Cracker Jack that some child had left on a park bench. I don't know which was harder: resisting the temptation to eat the candied popcorn myself, or dragging the box to my hole. Now I reversed my steps and brought the box to the storage sites where the food had been accumulating. Uncle Ninety-nine always put himself in charge of watching over the food supplies. I know I'm not the only squirrel who suspects that he samples the goodies before the circus. I even think he hides some of it away for himself.

After I added to the food stored in the tree holes, it was time for me to rehearse my tricks. I raced up my maple tree and jumped across to a neighboring one. The average squirrel can leap between trees that are eight feet apart. But I'm not your average squirrel. I'd been working on my leaps and was now confident that I could perform a ten-foot jump. I looked down from my high perch. Below me I saw PeeWee, half-hidden beneath some leaves that he used for camouflage during the day. I made clucking sounds with my mouth to call him.

Then I turned my head, and to my disgust I recognized the man who had stolen our breakfast apple. He was standing just a few feet away from PeeWee. I said that usually I can't tell one human from another, but after the bad trick he'd pulled on PeeWee and me, I wasn't going to forget this man so fast. What was he doing here? Was he watching for something else to take from us?

I shook my head to get rid of my angry thoughts. When you perform a trick like I was about to do, you need to concentrate on just one thing. I ran around the trunk of my tree to prepare myself. Speed is important when you make a leap. It gives you momentum, and to jump ten feet, one needs a lot of that. "Here I go," I shouted down to PeeWee as I flung my body through the air.

What happened next had never happened before. Instead of feeling a rush of air through the hairs of my fur, followed by the solid thud of my feet landing on the tree branch where I had aimed my body, my feet clawed only air. I didn't feel a branch. For a moment my feet pedaled the air and then I felt myself falling down. My tail acted like a parachute, and a moment later I landed with a hard thump on the ground below. I was stunned. I was certain that I could do that jump.

I didn't move. I lay in the grass trying to catch my breath.

"Lexi! Are you all right? Are you alive?" a worried voice shouted out to me. At the same time I noticed the apple thief rushing toward me. There was no way I was going to let him get his hands on me.

My animal instinct returned before the movement in my legs did. "PeeWee," I called as the man came closer, "get back under those leaves."

I stood shakily and ran toward the trunk of the nearest tree and climbed to the first branch.

PeeWee returned to his screen of leaves, but he was still calling to me. "Lexi, what happened? I never saw you fall before."

"Stop worrying," I called back to him. There was an unusual tingling sensation in my limbs, but I knew that nothing was broken.

I wouldn't have been able to climb this far if there was a break. "You've heard that a cat has nine lives, haven't you? Well, squirrels have double that—eighteen. So now I guess I only have seventeen lives left."

"Eighteen," said PeeWee, his voice full of awe. "I never knew that."

I moved up to a higher branch as I saw the apple thief coming toward the tree. Worse than the fright and pain of my fall was realizing that this man had seen my failure—and he had seen PeeWee too. Well, I'd show him, I thought. If he wants to keep watching, he'll see what I can really do—and it might help distract him from the knowledge that there was a guinea pig on the loose in the park.

He held out his hands as if to take hold of me, but I managed to scramble higher out of his reach. At the top of the tree I ran about, circling the trunk a couple of times. The tingling was fading. My limbs felt fine now.

"Lexi, don't jump. Rest a bit more," PeeWee's anxious voice floated up to me. But I paid no attention to my earthbound friend. I was going to jump and jump I did. And this time I made it.

"Bravo!" I heard a voice shouting.

I looked down and there was the bearded apple thief wearing his funny hat and clapping his hands together as he looked up at me.

I didn't need his praise. Squirrels have existed for more than

35 million years, and we've done it without human praise or assistance. It was all my relatives I wanted to impress, not this man with the funny hat.

I couldn't wait until the night of our circus. And I didn't need this man hanging around while I was practicing. Why didn't he just go off about his own business like all the other people in the park?

The stranger stood below me looking up for a while. Then he bent down and began to look around on the ground. I knew he was trying to find PeeWee. Luckily my friend had hidden himself well, so the man finally gave up and walked off. Relieved, I climbed into my tree hole for a much-needed nap. I could still run and leap, but my joints were a bit stiff from that big fall I'd taken.

A squirrel's day is divided between eating and sleeping. Most of our exercise occurs when we're in pursuit of one or the other of these activities. The running and jumping that we do happens while we're searching for our next meal or looking for a comfortable place to take a little snooze. But of course my favorite sleeping place is my own home.

I have a cozy hole in a healthy, solid tree. I've only lived here for a few weeks since my former tree was cut down to make way for a new children's play area. I was very upset when I heard from PeeWee that my tree home was going to be destroyed. But as my mother always said, *Even a bad tree can grow a good nut.* For a while, I thought she was talking about nuts. Now that I'm older I know what she really meant—that good things can come out of bad. I would never have gone looking for this wonderful new hole if my old tree was still standing.

Unlike my old hole, my new home is without leaks and drafts. And I've lined it well with leaves and put all my old treasures inside too. It's impossible to run around a park this large, used by so many careless human beings, and not to quickly begin a collection of lost objects that may become useful. I used to own a couple of books, but once I learned that PeeWee could actually read them, I gave them to him. But there are many other fine items inside my hole: two unmatched mittens, a leather glove, a very soft woolen scarf, a rubber ball, an old wallet, and many other small things that may come in handy in the future.

I nibbled on a dry nut that was in my hole. Then I curled up on top of the wool scarf and promptly fell asleep. I don't know how long I slept, but suddenly I was jolted awake. I heard the loud barking of a dog at the base of my tree. I knew I was perfectly safe, but still I was curious. I peeked out of my hole.

The barking stopped as suddenly as it had begun. But below me on the ground I could see a very large dog with something in his mouth. I ran halfway down the tree to get a better view. What I saw horrified me: The dog had PeeWee between his jaws.

CHAPTER THREE

PeeWee in Trouble

I raced down the tree, landed with a thud, and ran to nip at one of the dog's legs. But as fast as I moved, the dog moved faster—with poor PeeWee hanging out of his mouth. I decided to run back up the tree and jump onto the dog's back. If I succeeded and landed on top of him, he'd be sure to release PeeWee. I heard a moan come from my friend. If I didn't hurry, he'd be dead before the dog let go of him.

Suddenly I heard a loud human voice shouting out. The tone sounded like the command of a dog owner. But the words were ones I'd never heard before. There, running toward the dog, was that same bearded man who had been haunting us all day, the man who had taken our breakfast.

He threw himself onto the dog and grabbed it by the throat. I watched the dog spit out my guinea pig friend and run off with his tail between his legs.

I called out to PeeWee, "Run! Run!" But before there was enough time for him to make any move at all, something else happened. The man bent down and picked him up. I thought of some words my mother used to say: *Out of the hole and into the dirt.* Until now I'd never known what she had meant.

"Bite him," I shouted. But PeeWee made no effort to escape. He was shivering with fear.

"It's all right. I'll bite him for you," I called out, and tried to bite the man in the leg. Instead I found myself with a mouth full of his trousers. The man kicked out his leg and as I let go of his pants, I found myself flying through the air. I landed a distance away and, although shaken, I tried to decide what to do next.

I watched as the man sat down on a nearby bench. He put PeeWee onto his lap and gently stroked his fur.

"Jump! Jump!" I shouted to PeeWee. This was his chance to get away. But instead of moving, I could see PeeWee's body relaxing. He stopped shaking and looked very content to be lying on the man's lap.

"He's not hurting me. He's very gentle," PeeWee called to me. "And he smells good too. I feel very safe here."

I was scared for my friend, but angry too. "Why are you smelling him?" I demanded to know. "Come with me right now and I'll find you something that smells good and that tastes good too," I offered, hoping to make him jump down.

PeeWee still didn't move. "Don't forget—I used to live with human beings," he reminded me, "in the pet shop where I was born and afterward when I was a pet in a home. That's how I discovered that good people give off good smells. Nasty people have a bad odor."

"You shouldn't let yourself near enough to a human to smell them," I warned my friend.

"But this man likes me, and he saved me from the dog," PeeWee called out happily.

That was true, I admitted to myself. "But who knows what he's going to do to you now?"

"I'm not afraid. I know he won't hurt me." And as if to prove PeeWee's point, the man continued gently stroking him.

"He may seem good now," I said, "but we don't know what he's thinking. My mother always said, *Go dig for nuts, don't dig for trouble.*"

"Your mother sure had a lot to say," PeeWee replied. "And you're always telling it to me."

"You could do a whole lot worse than pay attention to what she said," I told him grumpily. "My mother was a very wise squirrel, and I've always followed the advice she gave me."

All the while we were talking, the sky above us had been getting darker. A strong breeze began to blow and the tree branches were swaying above us.

"It's going to rain," I told PeeWee. Even as I said it, I felt the first drop on my head.

Instinctively I began digging for a last nut or two to fill my stomach before it began to pour. I knew it would be a warm summer rain, but like any other sensible creature I planned to go to my home to keep dry. Only the ducks and the geese over in the lake look forward to rainy days.

The man got up from the bench and put PeeWee on the ground. He looked around and appeared to be a bit confused. He took his funny cap out of his pocket and put it on his head.

"This is your chance. You must run now," I shouted to PeeWee urgently. And this time PeeWee followed my advice and rushed, as fast as a slow, fat guinea pig can, toward his hole in the base of a nearby tree.

There was a clap of thunder in the distance. "I hope the man has a dry place to go to," PeeWee said, shaking some drops of rainwater from his pelt.

"Of course he does," I replied as I continued to dig in the damp earth. "And if he doesn't have a hole of his own, he can stay in one of the tunnels in the park. That will protect him."

"Oh, good. I didn't think of that," PeeWee called out as he slipped into his home.

"See you later," I yelled to PeeWee as I stuffed a fat nut into my mouth. Then, thinking better of it, I removed the nut and added, "Don't get out of your hole until I come for you."

I didn't know where the man was going or what his plans were. But in all the weeks that PeeWee had been living in the park, we had managed to keep him hidden from the human beings. It couldn't be good that this strange man knew he was here. And I was determined to do all I could to keep my friend safe from him.

CHAPTER FOUR

The Stranger's Breakfast

I don't know where PeeWee's rescuer spent the rainstorm or the night that followed. But I do know that the next morning he was still hanging around in our area. I saw him sitting on the nearby damp park bench when I raced down my tree to search for breakfast. The man was watching me as I came down, and he must have recognized me because he began to speak at once. His words were none I'd ever heard before. I couldn't make out what it was he was saying and yet somehow I sensed that he was asking, "Where is your friend?"

Of course I couldn't converse with him. And even if I could, there is no way that I would have betrayed PeeWee's hiding place. But a moment later there was PeeWee himself. He seemed to be utterly fearless in the presence of this bearded stranger, and he ran right up to him. The man bent down and picked up my friend.

PeeWee lay contentedly on the man's lap. "Lexi," PeeWee called out to me, "I can hear his stomach rumbling. He's hungry."

"What do you expect me to do about that?" I asked.

"We must help him get some food," PeeWee said. He paused a moment, thinking. "I know," he said. "Take something from one of the storage trees. You said yourself that there was so much food there that it was bursting out of the holes."

"That food is for the feast following the Squirrel Circus," I said. "It is not meant for hungry humans."

"He's not just any human," PeeWee pointed out. "He saved my life. I wouldn't be here if it wasn't for him."

"Wait a minute," I shouted. "Don't forget how many times I've saved your life too."

"Sure you have," said PeeWee. "And I'm very grateful. But this man saved me yesterday from that huge dog who would have chewed me to bits. I don't think he has a home. I think he's living here in the park like we are. And somehow I think we have to help him."

"*Stick out your tail and you're bound to fail*, my mother always said," I told him.

"Lexi, stop quoting your mother and help me," said PeeWee. As he spoke, he climbed off the man's lap and made a big jump (for him) off the park bench. "*Actions speak louder than words*," he said.

If I weren't a squirrel, I might have been jealous of PeeWee's strong feeling for his new friend. But squirrels don't bother with jealousy. The world is full of trees and nuts; that's all a squirrel needs, and we don't need to compete for our possessions. So instead I discovered that I was moved by PeeWee's concern for this man who had rescued him.

The stranger seemed to know that PeeWee would return, because he didn't follow him. Perhaps he remained seated because he was weak with hunger. I, however, ran after PeeWee as he hurried toward the three storage trees. There were several squirrels in the area guarding the food. "Tell them it's okay," PeeWee shouted to me. As if my words would be enough to convince those hungry squirrel cousins of mine to let PeeWee raid the larder.

Cousin Seventy-four began chasing PeeWee when he saw him sticking his head into one of the storage holes.

"Seventy-four," I called out, "my friend was just going to help make an inventory of the food we've gathered." It was a lie of course, but I was afraid he'd nip PeeWee if I didn't stop him.

"Is an inventory something to eat?" my cousin asked as he turned to look at me.

"No, it's a list of what's there."

"We don't need any list," said Seventy-four.

Meanwhile, with Seventy-four distracted, PeeWee had circled around and was trying again to stick his head into the storage hole. He seemed to forget that squirrels have eyes that are positioned in such a way that we can see some things behind us. My cousin took a flying leap and grabbed hold of one of PeeWee's hind legs.

"Ouch!" yelled PeeWee. "He's biting me."

"A bite is nothing," shouted Seventy-one who was nearby. "Wait until you see what Uncle Ninety-nine is going to do to you. He'll have you for dinner."

It was of course an exaggeration. Squirrels, even big fat ones like Uncle Ninety-nine, are mostly herbivores. Meat is not usually a part of our diet.

"Help!" PeeWee cried out.

"Okay, Seventy-four," I said to my cousin, "let that fellow go. I'll keep an eye on him and he won't take anything."

Seventy-four looked at me and then at PeeWee with a very suspicious expression. He couldn't speak because the moment he opened his mouth, PeeWee would be freed. Finally his jaw must have become tired. "Run along," he said to PeeWee angrily. "I know where you live. And if anything's missing, I'll know just where to go look for it."

It was an empty threat. None of the squirrels knew exactly what had been stored away for the feast. Most of them were so foolish that they would waste their time counting the shells instead of the nuts.

PeeWee and I made our way back toward the bench where the man was still sitting.

"Well, don't just sit there. Dig up a nut for him," demanded PeeWee.

I wasn't used to taking orders from my friend, but nevertheless I began sniffing the ground around me. It wasn't often that PeeWee felt so passionate about something. Every squirrel knows that *a nut underground is a meal waiting to be found,* and so almost at once I found an acorn.

I walked over to the man with it in my mouth. As I approached him, I became aware of what PeeWee had said the day before. He did smell good. There was something about this man that made me feel he wouldn't betray us. After all, he didn't have to help PeeWee yesterday. I once saw a dog turn and bite a human. This man had risked that possibility when he went to rescue PeeWee.

I dropped the nut on the ground at his feet and backed away. Then I watched as the man bent down and picked up the nut. He said some strange word that I couldn't understand and then he reached for a nearby stone. He used it to hit the nutshell. In a moment the shell was shattered and the man picked out the pieces of nut meat.

"Thanks," PeeWee said to me. "Do you think you could find him a few dozen more? He's awfully big and one nut isn't going to fill his stomach."

"One nut is better than a thousand shells," I said, quoting my mother. But I knew he was right. What would make a fine meal for a squirrel or

a guinea pig would never satisfy a human being. I recalled another one of my mother's sayings: *One acorn a day won't keep hunger away.* I'd have to do an awful lot of digging if I was going to try and satisfy this stranger's hunger. And all because he saved PeeWee's life.

Luckily the man got up from his seat on the bench and walked away. "Thank goodness. Now I can get my own breakfast," I said to PeeWee.

"He'll be back," PeeWee replied. "So we should collect some more nuts for him."

I knew Uncle Ninety-nine would be very upset if he saw how I was spending my morning. With PeeWee's help I dug up more than three dozen nuts. They made an impressive pile, and it made my mouth water just to look at them.

"What a nice treat," a voice called out as I was admiring the stack of nuts.

Even without looking I knew the voice. It was Uncle Ninety-nine.

"We have enough for the Squirrel Circus feast," my uncle said as he poked among the nuts in the pile and selected the largest one. He cracked it quickly and ate it even quicker. Then, as I stood helplessly watching, he took a second and a third nut. PeeWee had moved off at the sight of my uncle. Now he was hidden under a bush, watching the pile of nuts get smaller and smaller.

"Those nuts are for a very hungry human who rescued PeeWee from a dog yesterday," I said as I saw my uncle studying the remaining nuts. He was too full to eat another and too lazy to bury any of them.

"What a ridiculous thing. Squirrels don't give nuts to humans. Humans give nuts to squirrels," he said.

It's true that in addition to the nuts and seeds the trees provide, there is a group of humans who bring bags of nuts to feed squirrels. But I never think of humans as our prime source of nutrition.

"Bury these nuts for tomorrow," Uncle Ninety-nine said as he turned away. "And don't worry about hungry humans. Let humans worry about humans."

I certainly had no intention of burying the nuts that I'd spent the last hour digging up. And in fact, now I worried that some of my other squirrel relatives who were running around in the area would smell the nuts and come for an easy snack too.

Suddenly I had a good idea. I raced up my tree and returned carrying one of the mittens that had padded my hole. With my uncle gone, PeeWee returned and helped me stuff the nuts inside the mitten. I know that's not what humans use mittens for, but it was perfect. It just shows that squirrels are smarter than the people who use the park. We don't cover our paws, but if we have a mitten, we can put it to good use.

As the sun reached its mid-day position in the sky, the man returned. He sat down on the bench, and at once he noticed the stuffed mitten that was waiting for him.

He picked it up and then removed one of the nuts from it.

He looked around and spotted PeeWee and me waiting under a nearby bush. He called out some words, making the same sounds we'd heard from him earlier in the morning.

"He's saying thank you," PeeWee told me.

"So now you've become an expert in this new language too," I said sarcastically. But actually I was pleased at the success of my plan. It isn't easy to hide nuts from squirrels, and except for Uncle Ninety-nine, I'd kept everyone unaware of the meal I'd dug up. But now, watching the man cracking and gulping down the nuts, I could see they weren't enough. He'd need a lot more than just a mittenful of nuts to satisfy his hunger.

CHAPTER FIVE

The Old Wallet

The stranger put the now-empty mitten into his pocket. I guessed that like me he was a scavenger, saving whatever came his way. That's when I thought of something else that was hidden in my hole. I had a wallet!

The old leather thing made a fine pillow for my head. But I knew humans had another use for their wallets. Many times I'd watched as fathers or mothers opened their wallets and removed pieces of green paper that they stored inside. They exchanged the green papers for ice cream, pretzels, and balloons for their children. The wallet in my hole was thick with green papers. With it this stranger could get all the food he wanted.

I raced up my tree to get the wallet. It wasn't easy. I had wedged it into my hole and it was harder to pull out than it had been to push it inside. But finally I pulled it loose, and with one corner of the wallet in my mouth, I ran back down the tree.

When I landed on the ground, I looked around. "Where's the man?" I called out to PeeWee, who was hiding under a nearby bush.

"He walked away," PeeWee responded.

"Look what I brought for him," I said,

proudly pointing to the wallet that I had put on the ground.

Even before PeeWee could come toward me and admire the wallet, two children came running in our direction.

"Look," a little girl called out, reaching for the wallet.

I leaped toward her, but she'd already grabbed it.

"What did you find?" her friend asked her.

"You can't have it. It's mine," she shouted.

That was a lie. It was mine and I was going to give it to the man.

"Let me see," the little boy whined. But the girl wouldn't show him. She started to run with the wallet in her hand and the boy chased after her. I ran after them.

Luckily I didn't have to go too far. The little girl tripped and as she fell, she dropped the wallet. As fast as a midwinter wind, I snapped up the wallet. The little girl was crying over her scraped knees and the boy was laughing at her. But they both stopped when they saw me racing away. I ran up the nearest tree with the wallet in my jaws.

The children came running to the tree, but they couldn't catch me. I sat on a branch and chattered at them angrily. "Go play your games," I shouted. And after a few minutes that's exactly what they did.

From my high perch I looked around. Where was the stranger? I wondered. Then I saw him, pulling trash out of one of the garbage cans. It was a sure sign that he was hungry, but after almost losing it once, I didn't want to attempt to drag the wallet all the way to where he was. I'd have to wait until he came closer.

"What do you have there?" a voice called to me.

It was old Uncle Ninety-nine.

"This is just a leather wallet," I said. "Nothing edible."

"Then what are you doing with it?" my uncle asked.

If I'd thought fast enough, I'd have come up with a story to satisfy him. But I made the mistake of telling him about the hungry human again. "This wallet is filled with green papers that he can use to get food," I explained.

"Lexington!" my uncle shouted. I know it's never good when someone who knows your nickname calls you by your formal name instead. "I told you to have nothing more to do with that man. It's bad luck for squirrels and people to interact. I know your mother taught you that. You give a wallet to a man and the next thing you know he'll catch you and put you inside a cage."

"Why would he do that?" I asked my uncle. "If I'm in a cage, I can never give him another gift." Of course I didn't have anything else to give the stranger except another mitten or an old glove and a rubber ball. But neither my uncle nor the stranger knew that.

Uncle Ninety-nine shook his head. "I'm warning you," he said. "You will only feel regret if you give that wallet to a human. Throw it on the ground. It was lost by one human. It will be found by another. Squirrels have the good fortune not to need green papers in order to get their meals."

I scratched my head. I'd been taught to respect my elders. Never had I even argued with one in a conversation. But this was one time when I felt strongly that I was doing the right thing. Uncle Ninety-nine was wrong: The hungry stranger with the funny hat would not put me inside a cage. Even if he tried, I knew I was too fast for him. Besides, I was certain that he wouldn't try. I'd seen how gently he had handled PeeWee.

"This man is good," I reassured my uncle. "My nose tells me that I can trust him. And my head tells me that I should help him." If Uncle Ninety-nine didn't disapprove of my friendship with PeeWee, I would have once again explained how the stranger had rescued my friend. And how PeeWee and I now wanted to help him in return. But I knew this wouldn't be a convincing argument to my uncle. My uncle understood everything about his stomach, but nothing about helping others. I decided to try and speak his own language.

"Uncle," I said politely, "you're right. Squirrels can exist without humans. But think how they enrich our lives. We could live forever on the seed pods and acorns we find in the park. But isn't it a hundred times better that humans come here daily and leave the most delicious foods for us? Remember: *A variety among nuts helps avoid life's ruts.* This park doesn't produce Brazil nuts, or almonds, or cashews, or pistachio nuts. Without humans you'd never have eaten any hazelnuts or pecans—and what about macadamia nuts?"

"Ah, macadamia nuts." Uncle Ninety-nine closed his eyes and began to chew the air. I realized I'd said the one word that could distract him from scolding me. "If only I could have a macadamia nut," Uncle Ninety-nine said. "They are the most delicious of all the nuts in the world."

"But Uncle," I pointed out, "they grow thousands of miles away from here. Were it not for the occasional human who brings them to the park, you'd never have tasted one."

"Macadamia. Macadamia," Uncle Ninety-nine repeated again and again. "I must go see if I can find one right now," he said to me. "I love macadamia nuts more than anything in the world."

Suddenly my uncle could think of nothing else. He turned and leaped from the tree branch where he'd been sitting. He fled from tree to tree toward the south, where there are often people who bring nuts to the park. I doubted that he'd find any macadamia nuts today. They are a rare treat, and I've only eaten one of them in my entire life.

With Uncle Ninety-nine gone, I looked around and saw with satisfaction that the hungry stranger was walking in my direction.

It would save me the effort of trying to drag the wallet to him. I sat patiently on my branch and waited until he passed directly under me. I was ready. At that moment I gave the wallet a little shove and it fell from the tree and landed at his feet. The stranger looked up at me and gave a wide smile.

But at the same moment another human was running by. He saw the wallet fall from the tree too. Now he reached out and tried to grab the wallet away from PeeWee's rescuer.

It was quite a scene: A tall bald man in running clothes was yelling and chasing the bearded stranger in the funny hat. But unlike squirrels who spend hours running and chasing one another in play, this was not a game. These men were serious. Both of them wanted the wallet and all I had wanted to do was help.

CHAPTER SIX

Ruckus in the Park

The bald man was also a bold man. He quickly caught up with the bearded stranger and grabbed him by the shoulder. I could see it all from my spot in the tree.

PeeWee's rescuer tried to push the bald man away, but he was not strong enough. He called out in his strange language and the bald man yelled back at him in return.

"Let go of that wallet!" he shouted. "I saw it before you."

I was happy that the bearded stranger would not let go.

Some people who were walking nearby gathered to see what was going on. I had to climb higher in the tree as more and more people crowded around the two men and blocked my view of the commotion. There were joggers and bikers, walkers and skaters, mothers and nannies, children and dogs. There was yelling and shouting, crying and barking, and above it all I could hear the sound of the two men who were fighting over the old leather wallet.

It was amazing that an object that I had found in a drift of snow during a day late in the winter was causing such a fuss now. I didn't know what to do, but seeing two of my brothers running through a tree across from me, I yelled out to them. "Twenty-two, Twenty-three, call all the squirrels you can." I didn't have a plan yet, but I knew that whatever it would be, I couldn't do it alone.

Both Twenty-two and Twenty-three are younger than I am, so they didn't question my command. Quickly they raced off, summoning other squirrels in the area. At any given time there are dozens of squirrels in every corner of the park, so it didn't take more than a couple of minutes for thirty or forty squirrels to join me as I raced toward the fighting men.

At the same time, without anyone calling them, the park's pigeons came fluttering out of the air. They know that where there are people, there's food.

The dogs began barking louder than ever and pulling hard on their leashes as we approached. And the parents and nannies nervously grabbed hold of the toddlers who were not safely inside baby carriages. Some human must have called the police, because from the distance I could hear a siren. The sound got louder and louder, and then a police car arrived. I recognized it at once because of a dent on its rear fender. It was one of two cars that regularly patrol our section of the park. It drove right onto the grass with its lights flashing and stopped just a few feet away from all the activity. Now even more people came running to the spot. A police car meant excitement for them.

"Okay. Stand back, everyone, stand back," a loud voice called out as the door to the police car opened. "We don't want anyone to get hurt here."

The joggers and the bikers, the parents and the nannies all followed directions and moved back. But we squirrels came right on closer.

"What are all these critters doing here?" one policeman shouted out to another who was getting out of the car. "It's like a squirrel invasion."

"I've never seen so many. It's more than I ever imagined were in the entire park."

That shows that the policeman didn't have a good imagination or even good eyesight. What he saw running around him was only a small fraction of my brothers, sisters, cousins, aunts, and uncles.

The first policeman ignored us and pushed his way toward the two men who had stopped fighting and were just standing side by side looking at the police and squirrels. I noticed that the second policeman was trying to count how many of us squirrels were circling the crowd. Since we kept running around, it was not an easy task.

"What's this all about?" the first policeman asked the men.

"He stole that wallet," the bald man said.

"He stole your wallet?" the policeman asked. He took the wallet from the bearded stranger who, even if he didn't understand English, understood who the policeman was. The officer removed a piece of paper from inside. "Which one of you is Michael Ryan?" he asked the two men.

PeeWee's rescuer of course could not understand what was being said.

"Speak up," the policeman said. "What's your name?"

"I'm Thomas Boomsma," said the bald man. "It's not my wallet, but it's not his either. I saw him grab it and run. So I gave chase. I wanted to make a citizen's arrest."

"Okay, Mr. Boomsma. Who did he grab the wallet from? Can you describe the person?"

"Well, no. It wasn't exactly like that. The

wallet came flying out of a tree. I didn't get to see the person."

"Was there someone up in the tree?" asked the policeman.

"I guess so," said Thomas Boomsma, shrugging his shoulders. "How else could this wallet fall down from up there?"

"Michael Ryan?" the policeman called out to the people standing around. "Are you here?"

Of course he wasn't there.

"Maybe he's still up in the tree," said Mr. Boomsma.

"Which tree was it?" asked the policeman.

The bald man looked around him. "I can't remember," he said. "A tree is a tree. They all look alike." The onlookers laughed.

"What about a Christmas tree?" someone called out.

Meanwhile I ran right up to the big black shoes of the policeman and started chattering to him. My uncle Ninety-nine would have been furious if he'd seen me at that moment.

"No one was up in the tree but me," I told the policeman. "I found this wallet. It wasn't stolen from anyone." Of course, just as the hungry stranger couldn't understand English, the policeman couldn't understand anything I said to him.

"All right. All right," the policeman said, totally ignoring me. "We're going to clear this up. Get in the car and we'll take down a statement at the police station."

"Listen. I've got an appointment," the bald man said, looking at his watch.

"It won't take long," the policeman promised.

I hoped it would take forever. It would serve that bald man right. But what about the innocent stranger? What was going to happen to him?

I had an idea. "Surround the car!" I shouted to the squirrels. Perhaps we could prevent the police from leaving the park.

At once thirty-seven squirrels formed a circle around the police car. I watched as the four men got inside. Thomas Boomsma and the two policemen didn't pay any attention to us, but the bearded stranger looked around in awe. It was hard to tell because of his mustache and beard, but I thought I saw his lips turn up in a smile.

The driver of the police car started the motor. He began moving slowly.

"Jump on the hood of the car," I shouted to my relatives.

Instantly the hood and roof of the car were

covered with squirrels. I jumped on the front window and moved my tail back and forth, hoping to block the driver's view. But suddenly water squirted in my face and two sharp sticks began moving back and forth across the window, causing me to lose my balance. The siren blared and the car began picking up speed. One by one each of us jumped or were thrown off the car. We may have slowed it down a few seconds, but no more than that. The police car drove out of sight.

At that moment I understood the wisdom of what my mother had tried to teach me when she said, *Stick out your tail and you're bound to fail.* Uncle Ninety-nine had been right too. I had meant to do good, but all I had done was send PeeWee's rescuer off to jail.

PeeWee would never forgive me.

CHAPTER SEVEN

I Go for a Ride

PeeWee was waiting in his hole. His furry head was peeking out as he watched for me. Reluctantly I broke the news to him.

"What?" he squeaked. "The man was taken away in a police car?"

"Look at it this way," I said, trying to calm my friend, "now he won't be homeless. The police will give him a good meal and a place to sleep."

"They'll put him in a cage," said PeeWee.

"You sound like my old uncle Ninety-nine. A cage can't be as bad as all that."

"You say that because you've never lived in one," PeeWee responded. "You've seen the animals in the zoo. They're fed. They're protected. But they don't have any freedom. They are trapped in one space for all their lives. Here in the park I've been free. I wouldn't wish a cage on anyone."

"Calm down. Calm down," I told PeeWee, who by now was running around in circles outside his home, nervously digging little holes in the ground. "Maybe there's still something we can do to help the hungry stranger."

"What? What can we possibly do?"

I didn't have an idea in the world, but I wasn't going to tell that to PeeWee. I stalled for time, saying I needed my afternoon nap.

"How can you sleep at a time like this?" he asked me.

"Easy," I replied.

And easy it should have been. Between digging up nuts for the stranger and then lugging the wallet out of my hole for him, I was exhausted. But when I curled up to rest, I found that sleep wouldn't come easily at all. I kept trying to figure out what I could possibly do to help the stranger. If I hadn't thrown that wallet to him, he'd still be sitting on the bench near my tree.

Gradually I formed a plan. But I knew I'd have to take off at once, and without PeeWee. My friend has more spirit than strength, more ideas than energy. There was no way his short legs could keep up with me. So I leaped from my tree to one near by, and from that tree

I leaped to still another and then another. That way, by traveling in the air, I could keep PeeWee from seeing where I was going.

My plan was to look through the park until I found a police car.

"Lexi," a familiar voice rang out, "I'm glad to see you're behaving the way a squirrel should."

It was my uncle Ninety-nine watching me from a nearby limb. He seemed to be everywhere today!

"Hello," I replied, hoping he wasn't going to slow down my progress. I didn't have any time to lose in my search for the police car. But my uncle ran down the tree to the ground and I was able to leap across to the next tree and out of his view.

There are always a couple of police cars driving about in the park, but I wanted to locate the one with the dent, the one that had taken the bearded stranger away. Luckily, after a few minutes of airborne travel, I spotted it nearby. I proceeded toward it at once. To my delight, because it was a warm day, the front windows were open. That was essential to my plan! I watched as the car moved slowly through the park. I needed it to stop in order to jump into the next part of my plan.

At last the car came to a halt. The driver remained inside, but the other policeman got out. He walked over to a young man who had a loud music-making machine with him. Humans call them boom boxes. "Turn it down," the policeman shouted above the music.

The policeman who remained in the car watched as his partner spoke to the young man. In that moment I sprang from the ground and leaped through the car window. The loud music covered the sound I made as I landed on the front seat. I immediately jumped to the back seat. At once I could smell the scent of PeeWee's rescuer. His odor was still in the car where he'd sat just a couple of hours before.

I crouched down on the floor and nervously waited. Perhaps what I was doing was crazy, but I knew that eventually the car would go to the police station where the hungry stranger had been taken. I would find him there.

It took longer than I thought it would. The police car stopped and started many times. The two men spoke together a lot. Mostly it had something to do with the Yankees, whoever they are. I kept still on the floor of the car and the two policemen never knew I was there. And what with the motion of the car and the warmth of the day, despite my anxiety, I fell asleep.

I woke to find myself in the car, which was no longer moving. It was parked on some dimly lighted street. I guessed it was evening now. All the car windows were tightly shut and I was trapped inside. I scratched myself and wondered what to do next. Being locked inside a car was not part of my plan! In fact I realized now that I hadn't thought out my plan well at all.

In a panic, I began racing about in the car, jumping from the backseat to the front seat and back again. I placed my head against the windows. I could see outside, but there was no way for me to escape. There was even a small tree nearby. Oh, if only I could be sitting in it. A man walked by with two dogs on leashes. And then I saw a young girl going by with two adults. She saw me and pointed and laughed. She wanted to keep watching me, but the adults pulled her along with them. I watched as other people passed by too. Everyone was on the move but me.

I realized that my mouth was parched with thirst and that I was very hungry. There was nothing in the car for me to drink, but fortunately I found half a candy bar that one of the policemen had dropped on the floor under the front seat. I was so hungry that even the paper wrapper tasted good. But when I finished eating, I was thirstier than ever. And where was the hungry stranger?

PeeWee would be wondering where I was, I

thought. Perhaps he'd think I'd gone off to practice my routines for the Squirrel Circus.

Squirrel Circus! Would I even be able to take part, or would I still be trapped inside this hot, stuffy police car on the night of the full moon? Now I knew, like PeeWee, what it felt like to be in a cage.

CHAPTER EIGHT

A Man Named Stefan

I must have fallen asleep again, because I was startled by the sound of someone opening the car door. I sat up and listened to familiar voices. It was the two policemen who had brought me to this place. Two other people got into the back seat and the doors slammed shut. I scrunched under the seat so I wouldn't be seen. I sniffed the air from my hiding place on the floor and was overjoyed to recognize the scent. It was the hungry stranger.

"Oh, my skirt got caught in the door. Can I open it, please?" I heard a woman say.

"Sure," one of the policemen told her. "The lock isn't on. You're not prisoners after all."

The door opened again and then slammed shut once more. The stranger spoke to the woman seated next to him in his own language. To my surprise, she replied with those same funny-sounding words in return. I could make out only one word, which she repeated several times: "Stefan."

Stefan. So that's his name, I realized.

"My cousin Stefan wants me to tell you again how grateful he is," the woman told the policemen.

"I guess he really must be. This is the sixth time he's made you tell us," said one of the policemen.

"It's hard to be alone in a foreign country when you don't know the language," the woman replied.

I began to edge out from under the seat, trying not to be noticed, but my paw grazed Stefan's foot.

Because he was wearing sandals, he jerked his foot and looked down at the floor. A torrent of words flew from his mouth.

"My cousin says there is a squirrel in the car with us," the woman said.

"I guess your cousin thinks he's still in the park. A hot shower and a good night's sleep in a bed and he'll be himself again," one of the policemen replied.

The woman translated for Stefan and he replied insistently. I was relieved that no one believed him though.

I could smell the park before I saw it, as Stefan had opened the car window. The police car was driving across town using the road that runs through the park. I longed for my tree, and suddenly, when I least expected it, the door next to Stefan opened.

"What are you doing?" asked the woman.

I didn't wait to hear the explanation her cousin gave her. I wouldn't have been able to understand him anyhow. But I realized what had taken place. Even though the car was still moving, Stefan had opened the door so that I could escape—and escape I did. Fast. I'd gone to rescue the stranger and instead, he'd rescued me.

I raced through the park quicker than I'd ever run before. I ran quicker than any competitor in the Squirrel Circus had ever done. I couldn't wait to curl up safe in my own hole. I wondered if my adventures had reduced the number of my existing lives down to sixteen. It didn't matter. I'd be more careful in the future.

Now PeeWee and I had something else in common. We both loved nuts and the freedom of the park. We both liked stories and listening to the birds sing. We both liked running in the dew-wet grass, and we both had been rescued from dangerous situations by the same man. He was no longer the hungry stranger. He was Stefan.

I couldn't wait to tell the good news to PeeWee. Stefan was no longer a prisoner in a cage and neither was I.

CHAPTER NINE
The Newspaper Article

I slept late the next morning, and then spent much of the day leaping from tree to tree. I was back to practicing for the Squirrel Circus. And I was more thrilled than any other year that I was able to take part in the event. Among the audience only PeeWee would know how close I came to not being there at all. I was pleased with my workout, and it was good that

I had the chance to practice. Starting that night and into the next day and the next, torrential downpours flooded several sections of the park. Mostly I spent the time snug inside my hole eating the nuts that I'd stored for rainy days and catching up on my sleep.

Twice I went to check on PeeWee. I wanted to be sure that his hole was not flooded. Fortunately I had made him stuff it with old leaves and moss, so although his home felt decidedly damper than usual, there were no actual leaks. I'd once considered giving him my woolen muffler, but I liked it too much to part with it.

Fearing he might be hungry, I brought him a nut. He in turn gave me a piece of an old sandwich, which he'd found a few days before and had thoughtfully stored away. I left PeeWee's home feeling quite proud of myself. He was becoming very self-sufficient, and I had taught him how to be that way.

"I'm glad that our friend is someplace dry too," PeeWee said to me before I left. He had been very happy when he'd heard the whole story about what had happened when I went to the police station. I told him the ending before I told him the beginning. He didn't like the beginning at all.

Finally, after two full days and nights of rain, the weather cleared. The air was fresh and dry, and it seemed likely that we would have a perfect night for our Squirrel Circus. I was busy practicing my leaps when I heard PeeWee's voice urgently calling to me.

I jumped down from the tree quickly. But he wasn't in danger. Instead, he was shouting because he had something to show me.

"Look what I found on the ground near one of the park benches," he said excitedly.

He was holding a damp newspaper. I looked down and saw a picture of Stefan.

"Listen," PeeWee said, and he began reading to me from the newspaper.

Troubles Are Over for Mr. Trouble

Stefan Klopot, a Polish tourist who arrived in this country a week ago, lost his wallet, his luggage, and most important of all, the address of his relatives in New York City. Speaking no English did not make his situation any easier. He remembered only two things: that his New York cousins had written to him that they lived near a park, and that the number 9 was an important part of their address. Somehow Mr. Klopot managed to make his way to Central Park. Then he walked uptown from 59th Street passing 69th, 79th, 89th, 99th, and finally 109th Street. Of course, he did not find his family.

What Mr. Klopot, whose name in Polish means trouble, *did find was someone else's wallet containing several hundred dollars. This* other wallet had been lost or stolen five months ago from Michael Ryan, who was also a tourist in the city. At the time, Mr. Ryan notified the police of his missing wallet and departed from New York for his hometown of Clive, Iowa, a sadder and poorer man.

At first the police were suspicious about how Mr. Klopot came to possess Mr. Ryan's wallet. A Polish translator was called in and he reported that Stefan Klopot claimed that the well-stuffed billfold was thrown to him out of a tree by a squirrel. Police believe that Mr. Klopot, who was suffering from heat, dehydration, and starvation after several days in the park, probably hallucinated and has confused the actual finding of the wallet with the hours he spent observing the park's squirrels.

In any event, all's well that ends well.

Michael Ryan's wallet with its full contents has been returned to him in Iowa, and the grateful Mr. Ryan has sent a portion of the money back as a reward for Mr. Klopot. Even more important, Mr. Klopot has been reunited with his concerned relatives, who live at 439 East 9th Street near Tompkins Square Park. "We thought he must have changed his plans," said his cousins Irena and Eva. "We waited for his phone call and it never came. Since he has no phone back home in Poland, we couldn't call him to check. We are so delighted to have him with us at last."

As for Mr. Klopot, he seems not to be any the worse for his days of living in Central Park. Through the translator he repeated several times how happy he was to be here. "America is a wonderful place," Mr. Klopot said. "Friendly *people and friendly animals. Especially the squirrels. You have wonderful squirrels in your country."*

When the friendly people at St. Stefan's Church in lower Manhattan heard the story of Mr. Klopot's losses from his cousins, who are church members, they collected money for the man so he could replace his lost clothing and buy a few souvenirs to take back to Poland with him when he returns home next week.

Mr. Klopot has spent the past two rainy days visiting city landmarks such as the Empire State Building, the Statue of Liberty, and Radio City Music Hall. He also insisted on trips to several pet shops in the city. "We did not know that our cousin loved animals so much," said Irena. "But we are happy to take him wherever he wants to go."

Of course PeeWee and I were delighted that all was well with Stefan Klopot.

"I've never heard of Polish," said PeeWee as we discussed what he had read in the newspaper. "It explains a lot."

It certainly did. It explained why we couldn't understand any of the words our human friend tried to say to us. And it explained why he was living in the park. We were both thankful that he was no longer homeless and that he didn't need to be in a jail cell in order to keep dry and fed.

"It says he's going back home to Poland," said PeeWee sadly. "I'll miss him."

"Yes," I agreed. "I'll miss him too. He smelled good. You could tell he was a fine human. But after all, you still have me. I smell good myself," I reminded PeeWee.

"You know I treasure your friendship," PeeWee replied. "But you spend so much time up in the air with all the other squirrels. Mr. Klopot was down here on the ground with me." He sighed.

"I'll try and spend more time on the ground," I offered. But even as I said it, I knew it was an empty promise. Leaping and soaring are part of a squirrel's day. There was no way I could spend as much time on the ground as PeeWee would wish for.

"Come, watch me practice," I suggested to my guinea pig friend. "Don't forget—tonight is the Squirrel Circus!"

CHAPTER TEN

Squirrel Circus

That day of the full strawberry moon was a beautiful one. The sun shone brightly, and the leaves and grass seemed greener than ever. The entire park looked beautiful, as if the rains of the preceding two days had washed it clean.

I practiced my tricks and then took a long nap. It was a good way to make time pass more quickly. When I woke, it was already getting dark. By the time the clock chimed ten, the full moon was high in the sky and there was a grand sprinkling of stars, like acorns under an oak tree. All around, the ground was covered with squirrels. And not only were squirrels on the ground. Hundreds were sitting on nearby tree limbs. Old Uncle Ninety-nine stood on a high branch so everyone could see him.

"Hurray for summer!" he shouted to us all. It was a reminder that not every season was filled with the comfort and plenty of the present time.

"Hurray for summer!" we called back to him. The sound was overwhelming, like a thousand nuts falling onto the ground at once.

"Hurray for squirrels!" Uncle Ninety-nine shouted.

"Hurray for squirrels!" we echoed, and again the racket from so many voices filled the air.

"Let the races begin," he proclaimed.

Of all the activities, running is the simplest, and so this event was for the youngest squirrels. Several dozen youngsters who had been born in recent months lined up in front of a huge sycamore tree. When they were all in a row, Uncle Ninety-nine shouted out, "One nut, two fleas, three squirrels, go!"

At once the young squirrels were off. We all cheered for our nearest relatives. I had my eye on little Seventeen but I admit that in the crush of racing squirrels, I lost sight of him. It didn't really matter. There's never a winner for the races. Every squirrel is declared a champion. It makes them all feel happy and proud to be a squirrel.

Next came tree climbing. Only a dozen squirrels at a time performed. But the first to reach the top of the tree from each group eventually competed with one another.

There were many other activities that night too: catch the squirrel, hide-the-nut & find-the-nut, tree leaping, and as a grand finale: balancing. That event was performed both on tree branches and along the phone lines which were at the edges of the park. In addition to leaping, this is the category where I am a star. All the squirrels raced to a street at the eastern border of the park and I prepared to show them what I had taught myself to do.

I scampered to the top of the telephone pole and stood still for a moment before I began my performance. I looked down at the hundreds of squirrels who were watching. PeeWee was down there too, although I couldn't spot him. The street lamps cast more shadows than light. I could also see human couples walking down below and even a few dedicated joggers still doing their runs. None of them looked up and so none of them knew what they were missing.

I raised a paw to wave to my relatives below. Although I'd practiced all morning, I still felt nervous. I wasn't afraid of falling, since I still had so many lives left. But it would be very embarrassing to fail in front of so many of my relatives. I knew that this year I hadn't practiced as much as last. Lately I'd spent more time on the ground with PeeWee. But then I thought to myself, what were the few minutes of glory that I was hoping for compared to the days of pleasure I'd gained by knowing

PeeWee? Whatever happened on the high wire, PeeWee would still be my friend.

With that thought in my head, I started racing across the wire. Along my route I made any number of single somersaults. And finally I took a breath and ended with a flourish. I performed a daring triple somersault.

I landed safely on the wire without slipping. From below I could hear the thunderous roar from my family. I had made it! Few squirrels have ever been capable of doing a triple.

Back on the ground I was congratulated by many squirrels for my acrobatic feat. I was proud, but I was hungry too.

"When do we eat?" I called out to Uncle Ninety-nine.

"In a moment," he said, and he began counting out again: "One nut, two fleas, three squirrels, go!"

At once every squirrel raced off to the trees where the feast was stored. When I had a nut in each cheek, I went searching for PeeWee. He was not among the squirrels circling the storage trees. I finally discovered him outside his tree hole. I was in for a big surprise.

Standing next to PeeWee was another guinea pig. In the light cast by the moon I could see that she was very beautiful, with a golden brown coat and dark black eyes. Where did this creature come from?

PeeWee introduced me at once. "This is Plush," he said. "Stefan Klopot brought her here."

"Stefan Klopot. Was he in the park tonight?" I asked in amazement, disappointed that I'd missed him.

"Yes. Stefan Klopot sat down on the bench and watched the whole circus. He applauded when you did your somersaults. And Plush and I watched you too," PeeWee added.

I looked at Plush. Stefan Klopot had given PeeWee the one thing that I never could. He had brought him a companion of his own species.

"I'm frightened," whispered Plush. "I was living in a cage. And now I'm here. What am I going to do?"

"Don't worry," PeeWee told her. "This is Central Park. It's bigger and better than a hundred cages, and I'll take care of you." As if to prove his point, he began to groom his new friend. "Look," he told her, pointing to his hole. "This is where you'll live now."

I looked into his dark, damp hole and

thought of something. "I'll be right back," I shouted as I raced up my tree. From my nest hole I pulled out the woolen muffler that I'd been saving for myself. My hole looked pretty empty without the muffler or the mitten or the wallet, but I knew it wouldn't take long for me to find new treasures to stuff inside in their place.

I ran down the tree with the muffler in my mouth. "Here," I called to the two guinea pigs. "Put this in your hole. It will keep it warmer and drier."

PeeWee took the muffler from me and began to push it into his hole.

"Thank you," said Plush softly. "I can see you are going to be a good friend to us."

"Plush," PeeWee said, "Lexi is the best squirrel in the park. In fact I'm certain that

he's the best in the world. We're lucky to know him."

I looked at the two guinea pigs in front of me. PeeWee's praise made me feel better than all the applause of my fellow squirrels that I'd received after my balancing act. And, I thought, what is a somersault or even a triple somersault compared with a good friend?

My mother and Uncle Ninety-nine might insist, *Stick out your tail and you're bound to fail,* but I think they're wrong about this. I've decided that life is much more than leaping and eating and waving a tail. PeeWee doesn't even have a tail worth speaking about, and yet he's taught me to stick mine out. It's been a good lesson.

"Plush," I said to the new guinea pig, "it's late now, and dark. Time for all of us to get a good night's rest. But tomorrow and all the tomorrows to come, we'll go hunting for delicious things to eat and beautiful flowers to sniff and admire. You're going to be very happy in this park. I promise you that."

"He's right," PeeWee told Plush. "We will be very happy here together."

I'd have my work cut out for me: looking

after *two* guinea pigs. But I knew we'd have fun together too.

"Good night," I called to them both as they crawled into PeeWee's home. Then I ran up my tree to my hole. It was time for me to go to sleep as well. Tomorrow would bring us all new adventures.